D1537297

CoW on the Tracks

7

Cow on the Tracks

New Kids Media™ is published by Baker Book House Company, P.O. Box 6287, Grand Rapids, MI 49516-628

ISBN 0-8010-4486-3

Printed in China

1 2 3 4 5 6 7 — 04 03 02 01

CoW
on the Tracks

Todd Aaron Smith

BAKER
A DIVISION OF
Baker Book House Co

Everything seemed normal in the barnyard on this sunny fall day. Cow sighed dreamily as she chewed on a weed from the field.

The farmer was enjoying the day as he worked hard at mending the fence that surrounded the farm. It was a great day to be outside, and the farmer was very happy.

The farmer knew that some of the animals loved to wander around and sometimes they got lost. Cow especially loved to wander. The farmer told Cow to be very careful.

The farmer lovingly told Cow that it was very important to stay near the farm. "And whatever you do," said the farmer, "don't go near the railroad tracks just over the hill!"

As the farmer walked away, Cow stepped outside the big gap in the fence. She looked across the field toward the hill in the distance. How wonderful it would be to explore that hill! Still, she remembered what the farmer had said about staying near the farm.

As she stood there thinking, Cow was startled by a voice behind her. "Hello there, friend!" said the voice. Cow turned around to see a little red fox standing in the grass. "Oh! Hello, Mr. Fox," Cow answered.

"Would you like to go and explore the countryside with me?" asked the fox. "It will be great fun! How about it, Cow?"

The fox was still talking when Cow
politely answered, "The farmer said to
stay near the farm and to keep completely
away from the train tracks over there."
The little fox began laughing and said,
"Aw, come on! The tracks are GREAT!"
The fox was now jumping up and down
in his excitement.

The fox hopped up onto Cow's back and continued, "There is nothing that can hurt you at the tracks! I've been there many times myself! Come on! You'll see!"

Cow was very curious. The little fox might be right. At least it wouldn't hurt to walk along with this new friend. So she went with the fox to the top of the hill and looked down at the tracks below.

"Come on!" said the fox. "Let's get closer to the tracks!" Cow went a little bit nearer. She seemed safe. Everything was quiet. The farmer must have been wrong. Nothing bad could happen to her here.

"You see?" said the fox, who was now jumping up and down on the tracks. "It's alright! That old farmer just doesn't want you to have any fun!"

Soon Cow found
herself standing right
on the tracks.

Cow really began to enjoy her new surroundings as she walked along the tracks. She walked farther and farther away from the farm. Soon she forgot the farmer's words of warning.

Suddenly the fox's ears stood straight up!
Cow watched as the fox immediately stopped
walking and talking. He turned his head
sharply to the side. "What is it?" asked Cow.

Cow continued watching as the fox quickly ran off the tracks and disappeared into the trees. "Now where did that little fox go to in such a hurry?" she wondered.

Suddenly Cow heard a sound she had never heard before. It was loud and getting louder. Cow turned her head and saw what had scared off the fox.

A train was coming!

Cow didn't know what to do! She began to walk as quickly as she could. But it seemed as though she couldn't walk quickly enough. The train was moving very fast and getting very close!

Cow started to run. Her heart was beating very hard, and still she couldn't outrun the train!

Then, as the train came even closer, Cow covered her head and closed her eyes and held her breath, waiting.

SHOVE!

Just then, Cow felt two very strong hands pushing her off the train tracks to safety.

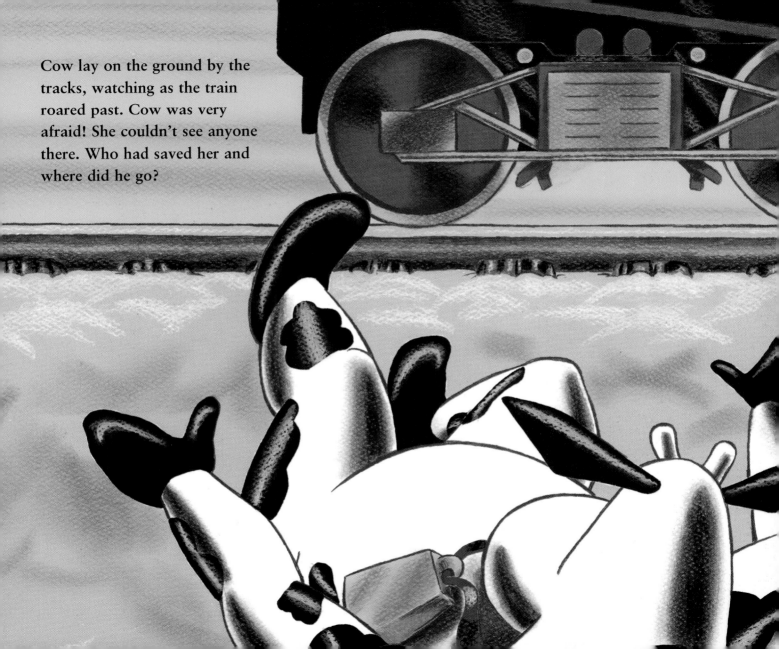

Cow lay on the ground by the tracks, watching as the train roared past. Cow was very afraid! She couldn't see anyone there. Who had saved her and where did he go?

As the train continued to roll past, Cow could now only think about the one who saved her! Where was he? Had he given his life for her?

Cow felt very sad. If only she had listened to the farmer and what he had said about those tracks! Cow was very sorry that she hadn't listened, and now she understood why the farmer didn't want her to go so far away, near the dangerous train tracks.

Soon, the train passed and the dust settled, Cow could see the farmer on the other side of the tracks! It was the farmer who had saved her. And he was alright!

The farmer put his hand
on Cow's head and said,
"I almost lost you, silly
Cow! If you would just
trust me, you would
always be safe. Let's go
on home now."

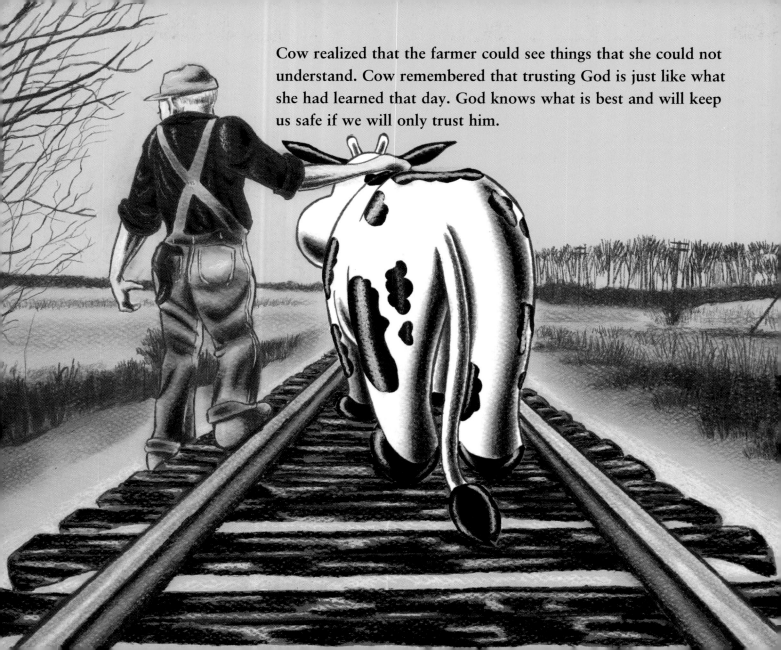

Cow realized that the farmer could see things that she could not understand. Cow remembered that trusting God is just like what she had learned that day. God knows what is best and will keep us safe if we will only trust him.

As Cow made it back to the farm, she thought about how much the farmer really cared about her. Cow had learned a very important lesson that day about trust, and she was very glad to be home where she was safe.

Cow never again went to the railroad tracks, but every time she heard the train off in the distance, it reminded her that God will keep her safe, as long as she trusts him.